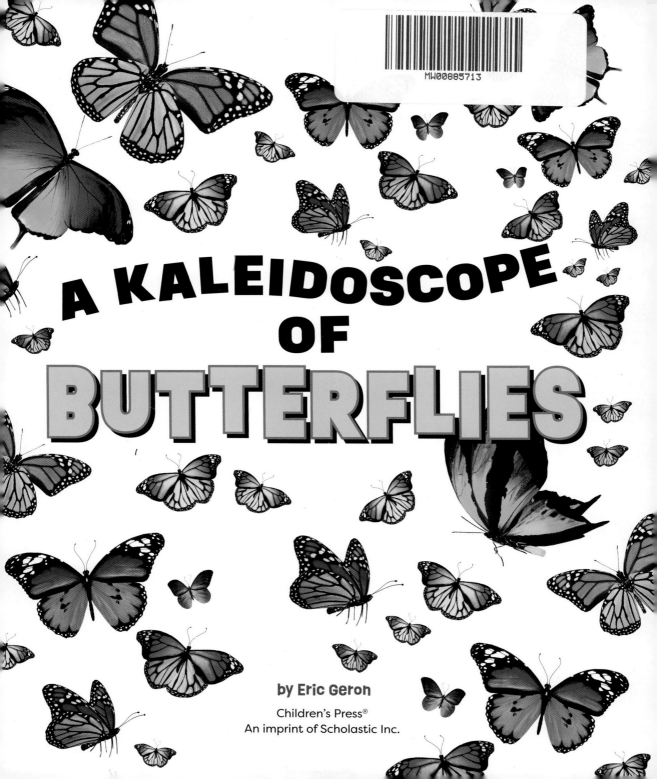

A KALEIDOSCOPE OF BUTTERFLIES

by Eric Geron

Children's Press®
An imprint of Scholastic Inc.

**A special thank-you to
the team at the Cincinnati Zoo & Botanical Garden
for their expert consultation.**

Library of Congress Cataloging-in-Publication Data
Names: Geron, Eric, author.
Title: A kaleidoscope of butterflies / by Eric Geron.
Description: New York, NY : Children's Press, an imprint of Scholastic Inc., [2023] | Series: Learn about animals | Includes index.
Audience: Ages 5–7. | Audience: Grades K–1. |
Summary: "Next set in the Learn About series about animal groups"—Provided by publisher.
Identifiers: LCCN 2022025178 (print) | LCCN 2022025179 (ebook) | ISBN 9781338853346 (library binding)
ISBN 9781338853353 (paperback) | ISBN 9781338853360 (ebk)
Subjects: LCSH: Butterflies—Juvenile literature. | Butterflies—Behavior—Juvenile literature. | Butterflies—Nomenclature
(Popular)—Juvenile literature. | BISAC: JUVENILE NONFICTION / Animals / General
JUVENILE NONFICTION / Animals / Butterflies, Moths & Caterpillars
Classification: LCC QL544.2 .G383 2023 (print) | LCC QL544.2 (ebook) | DDC 595.78/9—dc23/eng/20220606
LC record available at https://lccn.loc.gov/2022025178
LC ebook record available at https://lccn.loc.gov/2022025179

10 9 8 7 6 5 4 3 2 1   23 24 25 26 27

Printed in China   62
First edition, 2023

Book design by Kimberly Shake

Photos ©: 4–5: Sylvain Cordier/NPL/Minden Pictures; 8–9: Silvia Reiche/Minden Pictures; 9 top right: Kathy deWitt/Alamy Images; 10 left: Richard Becker/FLPA/Minden Pictures; 10 center right: Rinus Baak/Dreamstime; 10 bottom right: Robert J. Erwin/Science Source; 11 left: Photography by Alexandra Ridge/Getty Images; 11 top right: Universal Images Group/Getty Images; 12–13: Istvan Kandar Photography/Getty Images; 14–15: borchee/Getty Images; 15 top left: DEEPU SG/Alamy Images; 18–19: Paul Reeves/Dreamstime; 19 top right: Adisak Mitrprayoon/Getty Images; 22–23: Sylvain Cordier/NPL/Minden Pictures; 23 bottom: Ingo Arndt/NPL/Minden Pictures; 25 right: Thomas Marent/Minden Pictures; 26 bottom right: Silvia Reiche/Minden Pictures; 28 top: barbaraaaa/Getty Images; 29 bottom: Thomas Marent/Minden Pictures; 30 bottom: George Rizer/The Boston Globe/Getty Images.

All other photos © Shutterstock.

TABLE OF CONTENTS

WHAT IS A KALEIDOSCOPE OF BUTTERFLIES?

Many animals form groups for different reasons. Some animals travel together in groups. Others form groups to protect one another. Groups of different animals also have many different names. This book explores butterflies! Butterflies are insects. A group of butterflies is called a **kaleidoscope** (kuh-LYE-duh-skope).

Some butterfly kaleidoscopes can grow so large that they number in the millions!

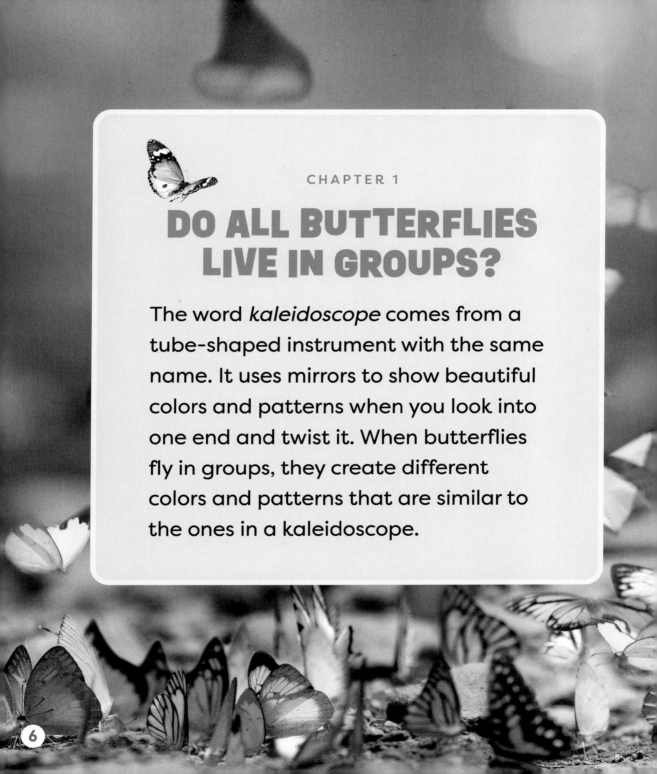

CHAPTER 1

DO ALL BUTTERFLIES LIVE IN GROUPS?

The word *kaleidoscope* comes from a tube-shaped instrument with the same name. It uses mirrors to show beautiful colors and patterns when you look into one end and twist it. When butterflies fly in groups, they create different colors and patterns that are similar to the ones in a kaleidoscope.

Besides the term *kaleidoscope*, a group of butterflies can also be called a flight, flock, flutter, rabble, roost, swarm, or wing.

How many different types of butterflies can you see?

Butterflies only fly during the daytime.

A Red Admiral rests on a green stem.

8

Most butterflies do not spend their everyday lives in groups. They tend to be animals that live alone. The butterflies that form groups do so to keep warm, find shelter, and find food and water. They also form kaleidoscopes during their **migration** from one place to another. Like many animals, butterflies migrate to find warmer weather when it grows cool. When migrating, butterflies start flying alone and form groups along the way.

Painted Ladies feed on flowering plants.

Some types of butterflies that travel in large kaleidoscopes are Monarchs, Red Admirals, and Painted Ladies.

Red Admirals

Monarchs

Painted Ladies

Mourning Cloaks

Cloudless Sulphurs

American Ladies

Other types of butterflies that can be found in smaller groups are Cloudless Sulphurs, American Ladies, and Mourning Cloaks.

There are about 17,500 **species** of butterflies in the world.

11

CHAPTER 2

WHERE DO BUTTERFLIES LIVE?

Butterflies can be found all over the world! Butterflies live in almost every **habitat** that planet Earth has to offer, from deserts and grasslands to mountains and wetlands. Many species can also be found in forests, including rain forests. Kaleidoscopes join together to find shelter in these different habitats.

These Blue Morphos flutter through the warm air in Costa Rica.

Butterflies form groups to keep warm when the temperature drops. They can survive in almost any environment—except for extreme cold!

Lots of butterflies enjoy fluttering in gardens and fields of flowers. These butterflies are not joined together in kaleidoscopes. They are each separately attracted to the many flowers that blossom all around the same time.

The largest butterfly in the world is the Queen Alexandra's Birdwing. It has a **wingspan** of up to 11 inches (28 cm).

Different types of butterflies can be seen together in a meadow of bright flowers.

CHAPTER 3

WHAT DO BUTTERFLIES LOOK LIKE?

The body of a butterfly is divided into three main parts. These are the head, the thorax, and the abdomen. Butterflies use a straw-like mouth, or **proboscis**, to slurp up sweet liquid foods, like **nectar**. The thorax has strong muscles that butterflies use to flutter their wings and fly. Each butterfly has four wings, two at the top (forewings) and two at the bottom (hindwings). The abdomen is where butterflies digest food and breathe, and it also contains their heart.

FOREWING

HINDWING

ANTENNA

ABDOMEN

LEG

HEAD

THORAX

PROBOSCIS

Did you know butterflies can taste food with their feet?

A Common Buckeye spreads its wings in the sun.

Butterflies use their wings for more than just flying! In the rain, they fold their wings together to get less wet. Or at times, they spread their wings to soak up the warmth of the sun.

Butterfly wings are covered in little scales that give them their beautiful colors and patterns. They use their colorful wings to attract other butterflies to them, or to hide from **predators**. Some butterflies stay safe by using **camouflage** to blend into their surroundings. Some butterflies' wings have eyespots, which are spots on their wings that look like eyes, to scare off predators.

Can you spot the Leaf Butterfly blending into the tree trunk?

CHAPTER 4

WHAT DO BUTTERFLIES EAT?

Some butterflies create groups to find food and water. Butterflies only eat liquid food. These liquids include nectar, tree sap, and fresh fruit. They also drink from rotting fruit, and sometimes even from mud or dead bugs! Once a butterfly's feet touch a food source, it uncurls its proboscis and begins to drink. **Pollen** sticks to butterflies as they flutter from one flower to another. When they land on a new flower, the pollen from the previous plant helps create more flowers.

A Tiger Longwing sips nectar from the flowers.

Butterflies are most attracted to flowers that are red, orange, yellow, pink, or purple.

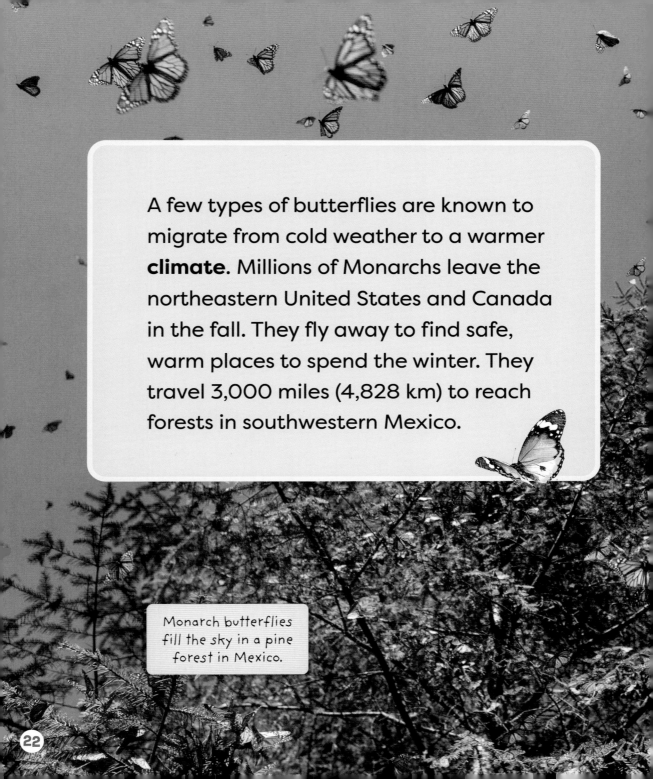

A few types of butterflies are known to migrate from cold weather to a warmer **climate**. Millions of Monarchs leave the northeastern United States and Canada in the fall. They fly away to find safe, warm places to spend the winter. They travel 3,000 miles (4,828 km) to reach forests in southwestern Mexico.

Monarch butterflies fill the sky in a pine forest in Mexico.

The Painted Lady can fly up to 2,500 miles (4,023 km) at a time!

CHAPTER 5

WHAT IS THE LIFE CYCLE OF A BUTTERFLY?

A butterfly lays eggs on the leaves of plants. An egg hatches into **larva**, or a caterpillar. The caterpillar feeds on the leaves of the plant where it hatched and grows bigger and bigger. As it grows, it sheds its **exoskeleton**, or outer covering. An adult caterpillar hangs upside down from a leaf or branch to form a **chrysalis**, a hard shell that covers their whole body.

This chrysalis hangs from a branch before becoming a butterfly.

Caterpillars can make silk! Butterfly caterpillars use the silk to attach the chrysalis to a branch or to create a "mat" to hold the chrysalis.

25

Inside the chrysalis, the caterpillar is turning into a butterfly! Some species take longer, but usually after 8 to 12 days, a beautiful butterfly comes out. Its wings are wet and crumpled. It takes a few moments for them to dry and straighten out before the butterfly can fly for the first time.

Butterflies can live anywhere from two weeks to one year. Brimstones have the longest lifespan and live for up to one year!

Life Cycle of a Monarch Butterfly

ADULT

EGGS

LARVA

CHRYSALIS

Marigold flowers attract Monarch butterflies.

WHAT'S NEXT?

Now you know more about butterflies and kaleidoscopes of butterflies. Butterflies make the world a better place and need to be protected. They help new flowers grow. They are truly beautiful sights to see. If you want butterflies to visit your home and the weather is warm, try making a butterfly garden. Plant some butterfly-friendly flowers, then wait and see!

Some plants whose flowers butterflies especially love are lavender, black-eyed Susan, coneflower, and marigold.

What Can We Do?

There are many threats to butterflies besides predators. One of these threats is **deforestation**, which is when humans clear land to plant crops or put up buildings. Pollution also puts butterfly habitats at risk. There are many ways we can help and protect butterflies. People can make a difference for butterflies by making sure they are not harmed. One way is to avoid using harsh chemicals on our lawns. Butterflies need clean plants and flowers to grow and live.

A Cramer's Eighty-Eight sits on a dewy leaf.

What Does a Butterfly Keeper Do?

Butterfly keepers work at special places like zoos. Typically, they work in a closed-off area with a garden. Guests can enter to walk around and look at all the butterflies flying around. Butterfly keepers answer questions and take care of the butterflies and their environment. They share butterfly facts with guests, such as information about butterfly behavior and diet.

A butterfly keeper spends time with Monarchs at the Franklin Park Zoo in Massachusetts.

Glossary

camouflage (KAM-uh-flahzh) a disguise or natural coloring that allows animals to hide by making them look like their surroundings

chrysalis (KRIS-uh-lis) a butterfly or moth in a quiet stage of development between a caterpillar and an adult; it spends this stage inside a hard outer shell

climate (KLYE-mit) the typical weather of a place over a long period of time

deforestation (dee-for-uh-STAY-shuhn) the removal or cutting down of forests

exoskeleton (ek-soh-SKEL-uh-tuhn) an outside supportive covering of an animal

habitat (HAB-i-tat) the place where an animal or a plant is usually found

kaleidoscope (kuh-LYE-duh-skope) a tube containing mirrors and pieces of colored glass so that you see many different patterns when you twist the tube as you look into the other end; a group of butterflies

larva (LAHR-vuh) an insect in a stage of development between an egg and a pupa, when it looks like a worm; a caterpillar is the larva of a moth or butterfly

migration (mye-GRAY-shuhn) the movement of people or animals from one region or habitat to another

nectar (NEK-tur) a sweet liquid produced by flowers that bees gather to make into honey

pollen (PAH-luhn) the tiny yellow grains produced in the anthers of flowers

predator (PRED-uh-tur) an animal that lives by hunting other animals for food

proboscis (pruh-BAH-suhs) the tube-like mouth of some insects

species (SPEE-sheez) a group of related animals or plants

wingspan (WING-span) the distance from the tip of one wing of a butterfly to the tip of the other

Index

ABOUT THE AUTHOR
Eric Geron is the author of many books. He lives in New York City with his tiny dog, whom he once dressed up as a butterfly.